Peaches and Posey's Big Adventure

Illustrated by Thomas Graham

Created with love by

Pamma

ISBN: 1-4910-1666-3
ISBN-13: 9781491016664

To the real Peaches and Posey who
are reminding me all over again
about the power of love.

1

Peaches and Posey were bored.

Mommy was working in her office on the 'puter and Dorisita was making dinner. The twins were supposed to be taking a nap, but they weren't even a little tiny bit tired!

"I know," said Peaches. "Let's go on a 'venture!"

"OK," said Posey. "Where should we go? And how can we get out of our house? I'm not big enough to reach the locks."

That was a problem because Peaches and Posey were only 4.

Just then they heard Mr. PeaPod ring the bell to deliver the groceries.

"He always leaves the door open when he brings Dorisita the food, so we can go out then!" Peaches always had good ideas. Mommy said she would be the death of her yet, but she was only just kidding.

4

Sure enough, Mr. PeaPod left the door open, and Peaches and Posey skipped through the door and into the elevator just as the doors closed.

Outside, they waved to Mrs. Gabriel who was sweeping the stairs at the church next door and walked up to the end of their street. They could see the park, but Posey reminded Peaches that they were not allowed to cross the street alone.

9

Peaches and Posey went to the park where the big bridge was all the time with Mommy or Daddy, but they had never been there all by themselves.

"So now what can we do?" asked Posey.

Just then a lady came to the corner. She was busy using her phone and didn't even notice Peaches and Posey.

"Well," said Peaches, "we can cross when she does."

And that's exactly what they did!

Peaches and Posey swung on the swings and went down the slide. They made friends with the little boy in the sandbox and played with his trucks. He told them his name was Ben, and he shared all his toys with Peaches and Posey.

When Ben had to go home, Peaches and Posey walked over to the fountain and splashed the sand off their hands and knees. Then they saw a lady on a bench and decided to see what she was doing.

They walked over to the benches and met the lady. She told them she came to this bench in the park every day and fed the pigeons. She said if she made a special sound, they knew she had food for them and would come to her.

"Would you like to see my pigeon family?" she asked the girls.

"Oh, yes!"

Pigeon Lady called for the pigeons.

"Coo-coo-coooo, coo-coo-cooo," she sang, and sure enough, pigeons flew in from all over the park! Peaches and Posey had never seen so many pretty pigeons! Some were all white. Some were all gray. Some had pretty green feathers, and others had pretty blue feathers like a necklace. Some had all the colors in their feathers! Peaches and Posey had never seen so many birds in one place! The pigeon lady let them toss some bread crumbs and corn to the birdies, and one pretty gray and white bird sat right on Posey's lap!

The girls heard the bells in the church steeple start to ring and realized it was close to Daddy time.

They said goodbye to their new friend and started home.

When they got to the corner, Peaches said, "Posey, this street doesn't look like our street. I can't see our building. We're lost!" And she started to cry a little bit.

Posey didn't like to see Peaches cry because Peaches always knew what to do, but now Peaches said they were lost!

Posey said, "We're not lost, Peaches! We're right here! We just need to find where here is. We can still hear the bells, so our house must be close. I know, let's look up high and we can see the steeple. Then we'll know where here is."

The girls looked up high. No steeple this way. No steeple the other way. But the third way, there was the steeple! They just were turned around.

It was Daddy time in their neighborhood, so crossing the street with grown-ups was easy.

Mrs. Gabriel's broom was leaning on the church steps, and home was right next door.

Their brand new neighbor was going up in the elevator to their floor, so they walked in with him. He was so busy finding his key that he didn't even notice the girls.

"Now, how are we going to get in our house?" asked Posey. "Well," said Peaches, "we could wait for Daddy and tell him it was a surprise."

But when the elevator door opened at their floor, Dorisita was taking the trash to the garbage chute.

"Quick," whispered Posey, and Peaches and Posey scampered through the front door, into their bedrooms, and onto the bed.

"Wow! What an adventure we had all by ourselves! And we met new friends and didn't even get lost, not really, really lost, anyway. Posey, you were really smart to look for the steeple," said Peaches. "I was a little bit afraid, but you saved the day!"

"Girls, Daddy's home," called Mommy.

Peaches and Posey were sound asleep on the bed when Daddy came in.

"They must have been more tired than they thought," said Mommy. "When I put them in their room this afternoon, they insisted they didn't want to take a nap! And that was almost two hours ago. I haven't heard a peep out of them."

"They are so cute," said Daddy, "I almost hate to wake them up, but it's dinner time, and I want to play with my girls!"

When they heard Mommy and Daddy's voices, the girls woke up and got their big Daddy and Mommy hugs and went to the table to eat.

So, Peaches and Posey, what did you two do today?" asked Daddy. "I missed all my girls today!"

Peaches and Posey told Mommy and Daddy all about their big adventure: crossing the street with the lady, meeting Ben, the pigeon lady, almost getting lost, and getting home all by themselves. Mommy and Daddy listened and laughed at their story.

"I think you girls should be story tellers when you grow up! That was quite an adventure story you told us," chuckled Daddy.

"No, Daddy! We didn't make up a story! It was really real!" insisted Peaches.

"Oh, I see! Really real was it? OK then, we'll have to put better locks on the door," said Daddy

Daddy picked Peaches up out of her booster chair, and then picked Posey up and tossed her up high. Posey giggled and something fell out of her pocket.

"What's this, Posey? It looks like a feather!"

"It is a feather, Daddy! It's a pigeon feather!"

The
End

Made in the USA
Charleston, SC
22 October 2013